Panoramic

By Aimee Nicole

Curious Corvid Publishing, LLC
Ohio

Curious Corvid
PUBLISHING

I love the way you tie me down
False words would never be allowed
When I am yours
When we are home

You loved the many faults you found
You kept what was worth keeping around
When I am yours
When we are home

Wanting you to know, before things become overgrown
There are reasons why I am this way
Wanting you to know, before things become overgrown
There are reasons why I am this way

I have opened my heart so many times
You have a hold of it now
I need you to breathe new life into me
You have a hold of it now

From: Hold
By: Vera Blue

For my sister,
who has also learned to flourish
from concrete roots.

Special Note

In a small effort to pay gratitude forward, the author will be donating 10% of proceeds to Day One located in Rhode Island.

Curious Corvid Publishing will also be donating 10% of proceeds to Project Woman in Ohio.

Hurt people hurt people, healed people heal people.

Publications

Sledgehammer Lit – Patterns
Vulneraries Magazine – Uninvited Guests
Borrowed Solace – Changes
Wild Greens Magazine – Direct Hit
Wild Greens Magazine – Prayers #2
Down in the Dirt magazine – Temptation
The Nonconformist – The Stage
Pile Press – Wreckage
They Call Us – Collared
They Call Us – Mining
Outcast Press – Sub Space
Outcast Press - Needs

Table of Contents

Uninvited Guests

This body is a dinner party for trauma.
The table is set at the historical cemetery in Tiverton,
on animal sanctuary land.
This way no one can ever make the overdue guests
leave.
They finished eating many years ago, but won't take
the hint.
I'm tired of entertaining so many needy guests at
once.
Picking up their dropped napkins from the floor, re-
filling their wine.
They are so amused by each other's presence at the
table and won't stop chattering.
How long have you known her?
How long will you stay?
Oh yes, I don't have anywhere to go after.
And this wine is very good.
I take short breaks in the bathroom, sure to lock the
door.
In the mirror I notice mascara running down both
cheeks in jest.
I don't remember putting it on.
I never put it on.
My fancy sequined dress is a fine distraction from my
puffy eyes pleading with ghosts.

A Break-up

This carnival ride cannot hold you,
in fact all of my rides need to be serviced.
Out of order for you, I had to find another
craving my freak show in the waking hours.
I demand too many prizes for your tickets,
sweat dripping off brow as you work harder for me.
Once I've had a taste of the highest ride,
I can't unlearn the thrill.
My tongue is still salivating for the next run.

A man

A man shoved the firework
of him inside my mouth,
massaged it down,
and detonated in my belly
smiling through his teeth.

I've been picking up the
pieces of me across Rhode Island,
shards sharp to the touch
cutting my fingers, blood trailing
behind me like a warning.

Changes

Your words seep through my pores like
poison cured carefully in the night.
Anything with a bite will do—quick and
sharp or a slow burn during delivery.
If I lie dormant in the bath floating just
below the surface, I barely feel your pinch.
Lukewarm water cools my
body's reaction as the minutes pass.
The ripples whir, surrounding senses.
I close both eyes and remember control
is being able to submerge completely and without no-
tice.

Resin

I'm ready to cast the mold
of me 15 years ago,
Lipsmacker frosted lips
and belted jeans.
Hair slicked back with
L.A. Looks
that made me look
like a frosted cake.
Dip her skin in resin,
be sure to catch every
finger that will bear brass
knuckles in hallways
hunted by foe.
Put her on the shelf gently,
she has dreams brighter
than an eclipse
and many rough hands
ready to smash that
young body to smithereens.

A friend convinces me to visit the plain clothes detective after school one day. The four of us pack into his office and offer the story of "our friend." A classic movie scene, one he's likely viewed before. Not a man of patience, he tells us he will call our parents if we don't give real names. Bait and switched after he promised to just listen.

My mom drives me to the police station in silence. I'm escorted to a room by a man tall as a skyscraper. He asks if I want to press charges. "I don't want this to happen to another girl," I offer. "Maybe some sort of educational program."

He tells me "boys will be boys." Won't let me leave until I sign a paper saying I won't press charges. Explains that this will never be part of the boy's record. My mom signs under my name and now I know my voice counts for less than a fertilized egg warming in the womb.

Re-assimilation

We watch funny fails and
idiots in cars on Friday nights
because this is 30 years
old and dating today.
Things have changed for me…
not just hairstyles but
the breathing pattern when
cops perch hidden on high hills
offside well-traveled roads.
Since our meeting,
I can laugh at the silly
cop shows on Netflix.
Unsavory recollections of
detectives tossing around
catchphrases to deter pressing
charges simply fade into
another girl's past.
On screen, Canadian police
argue with citizens citing
"trouble with persons"
and I maneuver your
thumb deeper down my throat.
A distraction and an invitation.
Look at me.
Look at how ready I am.
Come do the things to me
that I didn't want him to do.

Flattening the Curve

I wear the tip
down on my
dick lipstick.
So therapeutic
to wind it
up and apply
to puckered lips.
When the rouge
smudges outside
frame, I wipe
clean with pinky
in bathroom
mirrors…find
myself wishing
it was just as
easy to erase
the stain of you.

One Spring Day

In the cigar shop
city, state, district police
badges plaster the
moulding and I
wonder if that
cop ever thinks
back to his treason
when he breathed
boys will be boys,
ejected me from
the community with
a flick as if I was a mosquito
flittering around
in spring so hungry
for blood I didn't
care who I pinched.

Prayers #2

Standing beneath Echo Bridge
I howl obscenities into the ether,
hoping to crack a slither into
parallel universe, reverse life
before those wicked ways.
Hard to swallow but yes there
was a time when I didn't act
out for so much attention.
Sat in lace dresses on pews
and begged for forgiveness
of crimes I wasn't even sure I committed.
How can I confess every sin
when they are also the responsibility
of the boy who threw me into that
well of my mind until I could scratch
my way to the surface, knuckles so swollen
I required amputation at the wrist.

Advert

A felled spirit
in need of transit.
Bring the largest
transport available
for short term loan.
Gnashes on flesh
alarming, must be able
to hide acute horror
from visual/verbal expression.
Insurance required.
Does not assume
liability for damages to
equipment for any
reason including:
blood loss, mistaken
identity or perjury.

Shein

I retrieve a big-bellied package
jutting from the mailbox,
retreat upstairs and fish out
my plaid schoolgirl outfit.
Four pieces fall out—and I now offer to you a
pin pricked fingertip blood oath that
the description listed two.
There are no instructions
arranged inside the plastic trappings,
a dire foretelling of what's to come.
I slip on the crisp white G-string, then slitted
skirt that reminds me of my wasted
year at that Catholic girls' school.
The top is a wisp of fabric that
cannot hold my G-sized breasts.
I wrangle myself into some sort of
false hope that maybe if I just
manage to hook the clasp it will contain me.
As if on cue the hook zooms across
my bedroom and gets swallowed by the heater.
No matter how many times I try
to reconstruct those perilous days
trapped by his stare, the curse
continues its commitment to refresh
unflinching memory. Just once I want
to dress up these ghosts in discount garb,
make a mockery so they won't be
Coyote Ugly any longer.

Wreckage

I want a partner who will
pull me from the wreckage,
and will pull the wreckage from me.
So many times I've pulled myself
from the scene, skin burning
to a char. People hide in
the shadows, the stench
so rotten they cannot stand me.
As if the ruins I've become
are a contagious pathogen
ready to infect them with a wink.
I want someone to step so close
I can feel their hot breath on my skin.
Even when the danger is within me,
they will reach a hand straight inside
and risk transmission just to
save me from myself.

Baggage

How do I explain to someone new the baggage
I bring to this relationship?
It's only been a few weeks, but my suitcases are heavy
and getting wet sitting out there in the weather.
I can see them from the window,
dark shadows haunting the steps, haunting *us*.
Will you try to pack them back into the car and throw
them off the closest bridge? (Not hard to find in RI.)
Or will you bring them inside on a Sunday afternoon.
Unpack what's inside while holding my hand.
Lay all the items out across the living room floor so
they can live amongst us as friends.

Things you Stole from me

The Princess Bride
Sunday afternoons
Courage, for a while
Walking alone to class
Cafeterias
Football
Football players
Football games
Police
Calmly driving by the station
Humor in the phrase: "Boys will be boys"
One, two, three friendships
My relationship with my mother
My relationship with my father
Normal getting-to-know-you conversations
Intimacy
Faith

Journal Entry #2

Everyone waves tickets for entry but I lean against the fence, wondering why I didn't stay home with my kara-oke machine. Always content to write fledgling songs sprawled across the piss-colored carpet where no one can see me.

I don't know the visiting team, can't find my friends. People I've known my whole life turn away and shake their heads as if I've committed a crime.

I second guess every decision I've made since my first breath.

Maybe if I just…

If I didn't go…

Did I even say no…?

Time

They say even a broken clock is right
twice a day, but my clock doesn't even
have hands.

One Night Only

Tonight I cast myself as The Damsel.
This role is temporary and through nomination.
Makeup applied by steady hand only to be smeared by
costar.
Costume: negotiable.
Plus-sized lingerie to be removed by teeth (prefera-
ble).
Must be willing to endure all pain caused by props.
Must keep quiet under extreme duress.

Mop and Bucket

Our scene is your nightmare.
Was my greatest fear
turned to weapon.
Daddy, please knot
your fingers through my
hair until they attach.
I don't want to escape you
even though I'm always running.
Push my head down onto you,
keep going,
you know I can go deeper.
Push down all those
bad men until I vomit.
I've been cleaning up after
their behavior for years
and this time I want to
clean up my own mess instead.

Pressure Cooking

Please cover my mouth,
protect the world from my screams.
So many years of stuffing them down
like a bloated roast.
This body swells
—a marshmallow trapped in flame—
and nothing can relieve the pressure.
If my body will always feel like
a stew bursting from the pot,
sticking myself to the walls and ceiling,
please press down on my lid with all your strength.

Brickbat

Men call out to you
on the streets of Boston,
devour my body with those eyes
that overindulge in a glutinous feast.
They catcall how lucky you
are to have a woman like me.
As if these bulbous tits that
herniate disks equate worth.
Not the poems that ulcer from
wounds men continue to open,
an infection that never seals.

Temptation

Are you the fish caught on my line?
I'm too big of a coward to cut the artificial lure and
release you.
My selfish smiles back wages for all those scars others
left.
Our affair gazed with shiny wax but
underneath the skin it's just more bruised fruit.

Collared

When you click the collar
around my neck,
shake it twice…
be sure it holds.
Metal fits me better than
my favorite pair of jeans.
Hugs my veins as I twist to test…
how I tempt
with the ruse of flight.
Why would I
escape
your hold?
All my mistakes held
with a fist,
release every broken promise
with a whip,
say it's ok to fall—
how I don't have to
fail alone any longer.

Desperation

I put myself on display
an hour from you,
too far for rescue.
A glass doll peering
off the bridge,
one loose hand
fingering rail.
Is our connection
wire or string?
Will you know to
teleport in my peril…
or will this be the final
dance I tease?

Maybe I'm just screaming
out loud for you
to put me inside your pocket
where I can finally be safe and warm.

Exchange

Cement your lips hard against mine
and suck the pollution from lungs
until I'm gaslight empty.
Every breath today is toxic memory
fogging up this glass house.
I can't see two steps in front of naked feet.
Siphon this mess from
my trenches so I'm not
stuck in this poisonous
purgatory another goddamn second.

Trapdoor

My body wretches under starlight.
You slowly finger your way buckling wrists, then an-
kles…
planting sloppy kisses to skin as you work.
This full body bondage imprisons the body
but frees my mind to sink into vacant abyss.
In your capture I find freedom
having walked willingly into the trap.
I am both the lure and lured.
My strength strains the ropes while you
pleasure my tired body.
I don't want to escape.
I want the illusion of escaping.
I want to be caught.
Every suck, bite, slap is in devotion.
Our safe word, while not yet used, remains the
trapdoor
to escape my slumbering trauma, dormant just be-
neath the surface.

Mall Ride

People revolved
in and out
of days,
a merry-go-round
with many stops.
I didn't have
to try so hard.
Pushing the same button,
advertising the ride,
leasing space I already owned.
I really didn't have
to try so hard.
You were already enroute
and in time
for the final ride.

Vision

For weeks my vision has blurred,
chaos always dispelled outward.
Cavernous breakdown
of the spirit within.
I've spent years committing
the nuances of you to flesh.
Divots in skin answering every
open-ended question.
My fingers can trace their
way home to your lips.
I step into the black hole
of madness, having already
consumed you from the top down.

The Stage

I don't remember if the couch was an emerald fabric
chaffing my arms raw or blue-white patchwork like a
picnic quilt.
I don't remember if the curtains were soft see-
through
beige or heavy cotton closed off to passersby.
All I remember were your hands like snakes working
under my clothing, ignoring my pleas growing softer
then quieting.
The background noise of an unknown movie pushing
myself deeper into the pit of me where I would stay
for the next 10 years.

My best friend of long walks during sweltering summer days, Mandy Moore movie marathons, and pinky promises made long after lights flicked off noticed before anyone else. Observed once glowing skin now washed as needed. Body cloaked in black sweatsuits to float through halls unremarked.

Don't you understand? I was a glass plate in quick torpedo through time and space—inches from the floor. Confession to you would have been the rock kicked up to crack windshield. The one moment we watch in slow motion that causes everything inside us to shatter.

Your ultimatum was the prince's kiss, and I wasn't ready to wake up.

Being Burned Alive

Those damned papers made you feel
like you had some kind of right to my body.
Well I have other words now
besides "no" that mean get the fuck off me.
I am allowed to change my mind anytime.
I could be wound with wire, taped,
knotted in rope and my voice has *power*.
I could be choked with a plastic gag
and still flash my visual cue to kibosh all acts.
Papers can burn in a flyspeck candle's flame.
But my body can withstand sweltering
wax poured for hours and without recess.

Power

My throat has been raw for a week now.
I'm not sure if it's the Liga Privada No. 9
I smoked at the state park in solitary celebration
or that lazy Sunday morning when I took
all of you down my throat until tears moistened
lashes.
My body always bucking in protest
and defying orders, which I guess is the brat in me.
I've stuck my finger down there searching
for loose skin but cannot reach the culprit.
It's not for lack of trying I'm
always gagging after a good one, two, three
seconds then coming up for air.
If anyone's going to take my breath away,
it's going to be me.

Artifacts

I want you to reach inside
my cavity ungloved,
explore every cobwebbed
corner of mind.
Those forlorn memories,
expose them to the sun.
Lay them out on concrete—
the dealer who saw beauty, took a risk,
and sold old artifacts at the Saturday sidewalk sale.

Ruckus

This body is a
vacuum for fuss.
Causes such a ruckus
that requires immediate
and hasty mediation.
Without hesitation,
my butt inhales
the plug you inserted—
a prize it deserved to obtain.
Not willing to play some
catch and release game,
you were forced to
think in daddy ways.
Protection and care
upstaged panic,
you thrust your
hand inside me to
retrieve the naughty
steel piece. Yes, I knew
then, how you would
carry me across the
fire even when I set
my own feet to flame.

Permanence

I want you to lay down plastic tarp
and expel every toxin from this body.
Every misstep and errant thought,
grab hold and evict them by the root.
Make such a mess that the stench
displaces every neighbor into crowded streets.
I want skin that gashes, morphs into violet bruise,
something I can dare to transform permanent.
There are too many invisible wounds that
wake me in the night, please mark my
flesh to warn others how rabid I truly am.

Stretching

You guide me onto my stomach,
purple blindfold blocking out the mid-July sun.
It's still foreign, two years later, the
bondage of barbed wire fear gone slack.
Instead, anticipation wets, my scent
filling your childhood room.
The fresh opening of a lube bottle pops
and cool moisture primes me for probe.
The plug ordered is two sizes too ambitious.
Steady hands married with sweet praises coax it in.
Every errant thought vaporizes as my entire
system focuses on absorbing the pain for you.
There is no space in this moment to slump
back into old patterns of recycled torment.
Your presence demands my present and the only
submission required is the task of release.

Foreplay

Let me take the lead,
I want to pepper her with
compliments that reach
through Internet and
press hand to cheek.
We can exchange our tried and true
methods for deep throating
and favorite local sex shops.
If she wants a girlfriend to
browse the handcrafted paddles
at Mister Sister, will you lend me
out for just the night?
I promise to do no more than
share ice cream. Just a couple licks
between girls, no touching…

Feast

I send her messages,
please observe us quietly
from livestream.
Watch us banter,
send winky-faced emojis.
I know how your lip will curl
due north, cheeks flush
the dusty rose
that wets me.
Sit high up in the rafters
while we dance onstage,
a curious and familiar waltz
that teases from separate living rooms.
I salivate for the chance
to taste her as you survey
how I pleasure from the hotel chair.
A hands-off experience for you—
the rare chance to watch me
feast upon a body worth worship
besides yours.

Panoramic

Now that I'm not constantly
running from threats,
I take the time to evaluate
danger on a case-by-case
analysis, form strategy
before baring teeth
and taking the first bite.
This foreign feeling of
stillness leaves me wanting
to scratch that itchy
feeling until it alleviates.
Tame my manic
1, 2, 3 jump ways
by testing my will.
Stretch me with such
panoramic view
that even a map
cannot hold
every detailed desire.

A Letter To Be Sealed Immediately After Completion

Dear Daddy,
I put my vibrator down to write this letter.
Yesterday when you clasped clamps
to your own nipples, I sat protruding lipped
with hands unsure where to rest when unbound.
Lost in an identity crisis I wasn't sure how to
play, my switchy days misplaced as I flexed my BDSM
arm.
I tongued your lips, teasing the gag you had inserted.
Little hints of how I wanted my body pleased by you
when the roles reversed. I knew those few moments
were a rare gift and I was grateful for the flip once
the car sickness subsided. "See how safe you are with
me,"
they said. "Test my body until it breaks. I'll
always lead you to the edge…but I'll never push you
off it."
Maybe mutual trust was the only thing missing
for me until these moments we share.
Not a list of demands, but a chorus of needs being
satisfied.
Love,
Your Baby <3

Letting Go

Some days I want to float away untethered
from this planet where we procreate like dandelions.
Little monsters who fuck and eat and dream useless
dreams.
Gas me up like a blow up doll then pull the plug
and watch me whirl away with the breeze.
I want my mind to feel less like an unsolved Rubix
Cube
and more like a carefully crafted charcuterie
board that soothes your hunger pains.
It's ok if every rudimentary skill seeps from pores like
faded memories,
as long as you love my present self laughing wildly,
barefoot on the beach.

Ponderance

Maybe I just want someone else to carry
the heaviness that sits on my chest
like a brick house. It shadows all my
steps in tandem, wrecking my foundation.
Maybe I want someone to tuck me in each night,
making sure the blankets wrap
around toes so the monsters
can't bite them off bloody and kiss me
ravenous to deter my merciless nightmares.
Maybe I deserve hands that even when I cannot see
them
are familiar and feel like heated blankets
no matter the weather, never delivering
threats but good at fulfilling their promises.
Maybe I just want to cackle and not have
to contain myself, strangers turning heads
as laughter ricochets off grocery shelves
and you guide us through silent wishes—how they
all just want to don our sweeping grins.
Maybe it's ok to have emotions that steam
like hot water from the pot dampening
your shirt with me. Maybe I want you to wear me
everywhere you go so you never forget
the inescapable pleasure I deliver.

Detachment

During these power outages
when you are out of reach,
I'm thankful to have
two vibrators that thrive
off disposable batteries
rather than tangled cords
requiring fickle electricity.
We still cannot solve
this issue in 2021
of lapsed resources
that aren't even renewable
and do not damage the Earth
with such destruction
it is better off without us.
I ponder this in the dark at
3PM and wonder:
does your mind
race the hamster wheel,
questioning if you would
be better off without my
chaos and unmoored mind.

Overripe

Fruit aged and fallen from the vine,
I lay directly in your path.
You have no choice but to
pick me up, bruised,
press me to puckered lip.
My juices stream down
your chin and quench a thirst
suddenly ravenous and foreboding.
You wonder: *how could something so
ailing cure my own afflictions?*
Yet here I am, healing you from
bones to vessels to lymph nodes,
—ferrying inside quick as a cancer—
sealing up your oozing wounds.

Journal Entry #4

Those eyes gleam like a hunter's across the lunch-room…track my every move. My breaths are measured, shallow inhales and silent exhales, that only the dead can hear. This interest in me is amusing, our past such a cat and mouse game of me wanting your attention and you fairly fickle in parceling it out. How quickly the roles are reversed once I realize that I was the prey this whole time.

Patterns

When you
tug o' war
so careless
my emotions fray
like chewed through wire.
Brain so
rug burned
by that abrasive
tone and I don't know
if I should cry or
time out in the corner.
Don't you know
that flippant
style is like a home,
I bury my nuts there
and cannot find them…
every winter
I starve myself
all over again.

Guardian

My knuckles are bloodied and swollen
from protecting myself all these years.
Swinging in the dark at enemies
selling themselves in bulk on discount.
With one round left I'm dragging
myself towards the bench, legs limp and trailing.
I want a guardian, inviting rest like
it's time for my hibernation.
Make this bed comfortable
enough for me to strip down
to nothing but mending bones.
I'm putting down my armor
and trusting that you'll
remedy every lesion by hand.

Aftercare #2

Now let me crawl into that
place my head rests,
mouth opens to take nipple.
Do you know how your life
sustains mine?
My leg crosses over yours,
finds a home to blanket
the part of you which gave
me pleasure just seconds ago.
Our bodies dewy with
sweat, chests rising in tandem.
Just keep your arm
wrapped around me
like I'm a burrito about to burst.
Because I am, still settling, after impact.

Swinging

Even in winter
I swing on the same swing
higher than suggested.
Strangers look on
concerned.
Yet, they continue on,
not troubled enough to stop me.
The metal frame shakes
with the weight of me.
You were the first
one to stop,
lay down
underneath me,
say it's ok if you fall.

Direct Hit

As we enter hurricane season,
the first storm barrels towards us.
Rhode Islanders clear
shelves of milk, bread, and eggs.
How they plan to prepare a dozen
eggs once the power sputters out,
no one can answer me.
I sit calmly with electronics
drained—so many years spent
limbs flailing and debris blurring vision
trying to feel my way towards safe
haven center. I'm here to report
that no amount of preparation
can save your body from
the impending destruction
caused by a direct hit.

Needs

Today I need you to
take my hand and
lead me. Gentle reminders
that don't feel like
delicious temptation
to break rules
or run from you,
tuck behind curtains
until you find me.
Today let me drift asleep at noon
with your arms caging me,
protection from that
crack gaping
mattress and wall.
Today I need grilled cheese
sandwiches served on
plates the size of an island,
ice cream cones with three scoops,
and please drive me everywhere
like I'm a newborn baby
so precious the world is
foaming at the mouth for me.

Senior Special

It's a Friday night
during another
fucking heatwave
in New England.
Too hot to take leftovers
from the fridge to plate.
Better to drive in the
air conditioning
10 minutes west
for a hometown waitress
to pretend she likes
us for a while.
She asks me if I
want my pizza "crispy"
because there is a button
in the back she can press
to make it that way.
I politely say yes and
realize I'm spending
an hour's paycheck on
frozen pizza to be heated
in a convection oven.
The Keno cards and
clientele should have
clued me in, a bartop
crowded with older women
sipping Chardonnay, twirling
bleached blonde hair between

fingers. Men bantering
with strangers gulping beer
straight from the bottle.
We don't talk much
during dinner—I'm cranky
from the heat, my
unpleasured butt
sticking to the chair.
I leave my print behind
upon departure
for the next guest to
ponder who doesn't wear panties
at senior hour.

Suspension

Each inhale today
has been the most arduous task.
This body has lost all
reflex memory. Movements
are baby steps, I can barely manage
them one after the other.
Since birth the message repeats
mind over matter
but what am I to do when
my mind dissolves into a thick tar
sludge that just clogs up the rest of me?
Please eliminate the senses until I feel
like I'm floating in vacuous space
among nothing and no one.
Clip my memories free like
leaves that naturally break from
their branch in September so when I
come back to you this burden
does not feel quite so heavy.

Sub Space

Carefully submerge me
so far underneath the surface
I cannot rise until
your voice pulls
me up by the throat.
This skin requires
firm holds
that cannot be broken
by strong winds.
Can you handle
my fickle ways?
One moment demanding
a bruise on the hip,
the next a chest to
bury head so far
into I'm hoping to disappear
until reincarnated life
as a butterfly
floating from one moment
to next.

Mining

Allowing myself
to cum on fingers
that dig into
the cavern of me
—like a mine
full of jewels—
is the ultimate act
of submission.

Crayola

Take those markers
from the box
and write every filthy
word across chest.
Weave double negative
to erase crimes
others inflicted
through closed eyes
and raised fists.
I don't want the curses
to wash away
until you rinse wet
a washcloth under
moonlight to
cleanse me of
all the harm I've
suffered before
we met that fall.

Solvency

The presenter on this Zoom call
has a paddle hanging on the bookshelf
behind him, and my focus is obscured.
Body bending in anticipation of your
expectation that I curve to accept you.
How willing I am to accommodate
your presence when you are not present.
Sighted to absorb the extensions of you
reaching tendrils across state lines.
My body continues to recruit the potential
of pleasure, a hybrid investment of
fantasy and active devotion.

Sacrifice

Pass the collection basket
so I can enter my offering—
I've been saving up for a lifetime.
Dressed in Sunday's finest,
this body is on display
for your viewing pleasure.
Are our prayers being answered
or lifted to the heavens through sunburnt lips?
The vessel of me crossed from burden
to burden to bear, let me carry your sins.
Are you ready to sacrifice this flesh,
if only so we can be eternally freed?

Evolution

The most valuable lesson
you've taught me is that
maybe some people
are just looking for
mediocre conversation.
Maybe they don't have knives
hidden through
belt loops looking
to leave more
scars on this skin.

Aren't we
all just stumbling
through Mondays…
trying to pocket
paychecks and starve off
pesky bill collectors with our
extensions on speed dial.

Hurt people hurt people
and I've hurt people too.
I've detonated bridges
to nothing but ruble.
Lit matches just to see the flame.
Held my hand under running
water until singed.
And I didn't feel a damn thing.

Journal Entry #5

I am a jellyfish caught by a current. Surrender myself to the stream and float belly-up, legs trailing behind me limp as noodles.

How long this continues, I cannot say. Weeks, months, years?

I wish you would ask me how I am. Crack open some pearl of a conversation that sparks mild electricity back into my veins.

Instead, you ask if I'm on drugs. Abrasive words that scourge the throat. Twist you into a villain sleeping two doors away.

I slam the door between us, and it stays closed for the rest of our days.

Lawmaking

There is no need to puncture,
for I have bled many times
and that metallic scent turns my
stomach like sour milk.
Skin threaded until
the needle can no longer break
through pockmarked barrier.
An invasion threatening every cell,
lying in wait below choppy surface.
Even still, this is my negotiation—
the strength baring from a pack
of wolves offering my words
as law—my skin will not be broken.

Deprivation

I am malleable as Playdoh.
Pliable, eager to please.
Kneeling on knees,
splinters that tease.
Squishy foam earplugs
wrest from canal
and flop onto the floor.
Will I be punished?
I can't see through this tattered
bandana I'm certain you
picked up at a country flea.
I can hear you creaking
across floorboards.
The crinkling of a water bottle,
drops drip down my chin, chest.
You pull me up onto the bed.
I hear chipmunks screaming outside
and am jealous that they can
raise their voices louder than me.

Frida Kahlo

I don't take lovers abroad
when jealousy flares like a rash,
lips pursed to conceal pearls
rolling on tongue.
No, I became collared
unceremoniously and without protest.
See the one who clasped the jewels
is not who leads but who is lead.
Full-bodied and nude under
stiff, starchy sheets.
Always gowned and painted
to turn on my own mirrored reflection.
Our spines stiff like ironing boards
in the springtime rain,
drinking tea bent over
kitchen countertops again.
Two hearts beating wild
and somewhat out of tune.
You'll always be panting on the path behind,
we are ravenous for the feed.

Time Share

I can feel myself developing
bad habits like a teenager
away from home for the first time.
Acts of rebellion to gain attention.
How quickly I sink back into
these old patterns of survival,
so willing to turn on myself like
a pack of wolves at feeding time.
Sit in my filth to stink up the world
around me, reminders of its betrayals.
Lipstick smears cigars soaking tips,
always leaving my trails.
It's so hard to sit in a room
and bleed out while everyone turns away,
maybe if I let out a roar that claims
you as property, this trauma
will finally be shared.

Haunted House

I'm not old enough to be left alone.
Too many ghosts in the attic
waiting for you to depart
so they can launch their attack.
Closets are full of monsters toeing the
steel track…can't you see them?
Sharp corners catch my hip
and I cut myself on butter knives.
I eat grocery store sheet cake
for dinner over the sink in five swallows.
My brain is a functioning Escape Room
and the final clue is our bodies
searching each other for all the reasons
why we were even apart in the first place.

The Ghoul

I skip through days
with neon tights and a smile
plastered across baby face.
He buries that elixir
deep within me
upon command.
Did trauma seep from my pores
like a fever treated by
cold compress?
Or is it just the ghoul in the attic,
playing poker and smoking a cigar
slowly passing the years
until you leave
(as they all do)
to begin the feast upon
this rotting corpse once again.

Feral

You're going to have to
catch me by the scruff
on my neck,
teeth sharp and
gleaming in the night.
So used to running
from the oncoming
traffic quick to slaughter…
I don't know how to
slow down, feet calloused
by pavement.
I'm sure to ruin
everything you love,
wreck it from
the inside out.
A true catalyst to make
you wonder if any
wild thing can
ever be tamed at all.

The Male Fiddler Crab

I spend the morning searching
for our sleeping position online.
I can't find our interlaced limbs anywhere
in the cartoon photographs.
Every night I sleep resting head atop your chest,
an impenetrable barrier to block nightmares.
One arm winds around the back of me,
your hand clasping my throat
through darkest hours.
Fingers that buoy.
I've got you weighted while you rest, they whisper.
Don't step one foot into the bait of those memories.

Little Ways

Another May day drags us by the hair.
Rained out baseball games
keep us inside, pulling
covers to unpainted lashes.
Your toes tickle operated heel
and I don't want to leave in the morning.
Time builds in a deranged promise
to break like a tossed egg onto the structure of us.
Our parting always leaves quite
the mess for me to clean up…
you forever quick to hand over cleaning supplies.
In my room, I hug the stuffed unicorn
you gifted between bulbous thighs.
A quiet replacement for the
comforting stroke of hair
or kiss to shiny forehead.
I sit quietly and not without complaint.
Not until I can rest my head on your chest again,
smell that gamy scent of sweat
that sticks to you like a tick.

Fantasy

Strangers like photographs of me online,
a full-bodied offering to wet appetites
but never satiate. Mouth bound in fuscia tape
that creates the illusion of restraint.
How kind it is peeling gently from hair.

But, just once, I would like for you
to tear that tape from my body
with such force that it rips
cells alive and screaming, taking some
of the most stubborn memories with them.

Exposure #2

My strawberry crop top dips
low, teasing a peek
at the blemishes
marking both breasts.
Just one dropped fork
and all our hidden pleasures
will be exposed to those
universes milling around us.
If I bend over, do the cameras
screening our lives for profit
scan the metal you inserted
inside of me just minutes ago?
The shift from shielding secrets
is seamless. A youth elapsed by
calloused hands building barriers.
Shame knitting me inside that
suffocating net unseen.
Today, so aroused by the
possibility of being pinched
by the public in this game.

I'll Never Grow Up

When I bask greedily under
shower stream upon return
after our parting, it's not
to cleanse you from memory.
Immediately, I begin the
priming ritual to become
your blank canvas once again.
I thumb fresh marks
from you, unsatisfied.
Wanting you to push up
behind me, grab my waist
so firm I cannot turn.
How I wish you would
order me down onto knees
to take you down the throat
while water blurs my vision.
Left with fragmented fantasies
I know could be true
if we weren't separated by this
pesky state line and your
Peter Pan tendencies
that choke me behind the scenes.

Prayers

Are you going to take me away from here?
The roads where I drive past haunted houses,
spookiest in the burning August sun.
Will you haul all my old possessions, weeded
to remove every tainted trace of corrupted past.
Take photographs of me flashing incisors and tits
at your Polaroid during rest stops along 95S
because all I am proud of is this dancing corpse.
It's true, all I have to offer you are my
confessions and resistance and bags filled
with promises I've a millionaire chance of keeping.

Allegory

I am a dog that does tricks for you.
Every morning at 8, I sit at the door.
Whining for your permission to relieve.
When you don't wake in time I make a mess
and always get an earful for your error.
I act out by ripping up the sheets.
All I want are your hands on my
back and you yell for that too.
Why can't I just have soft hands consoling me
for the worried thoughts scurrying around this brain?
Can't you see all I do is travel from
one room to the next matching your steps with mine?
You are not my universe but my stars —
breathtaking light that charts my path home.

Perilous Paths

Today, I drive home in the hurricane
because I needed to feel you stretch
this body for hours. Having begged you
to switch plugs in my brattiest voice,
my punishment was being upgraded to the largest size
available for order with faux-fur tail.

I'm so used to this hydroplane feeling,
I grip the steering wheel
with one hand and let my Corolla
guide me gently down abandoned roads,
sipping tea that balances on leg pressed to gas.

F150's speed by and I let them pass,
aware that a steady pace assures safe
passage through perilous paths.
Instincts whittled by friends turned adversary—
for those you invite into your home who bring
knives into beds will always fork your path.

College was a fresh start, far from the threat of him.

College was a fresh start, full of fresh new threats.

For years I walked head down. Slithered along walls. Ate lunch alone during the opening dining hour. Refused every invitation to parties knowing exactly what those couches promised.

Walks were expedited quests to destination. Even in daytime under burning sun, especially then.

Sage

Late into the night,
I wake you.
Imposter syndrome
grabbing me by the neck
and I need you to scare it
back into the shadows.
Wrap both hands
(big enough to carry
daemons) around throat
until I can't breathe.
A diversion that dilutes
the traffic of memory.
I won't find rest again
until you've cleared my
path forward and dreams
seem like less of a burden
to overcome in the witching-hour.

Orbit

My tits are two of the largest
planets this solar system
has ever seen. Discovered by men
first, then women, as typical
by state-funded exploration.
You'll need to use all five senses
to truly probe the beauty of them.
It's open season and you're the
only guest I've sold a ticket to.
All other hands
harsh like sandpaper,
hotter than flame.
I'm hoping to lure you
into their gravitational pull
so you are caught by
my orbit for many moons.

Departure

Nights your toes don't kiss mine beneath sheets
I paint Atlas Cedarwood across upper lip to ground,
lullaby myself asleep with enchanting YouTube
playlists.
I work myself down a list of tricks like I'm five years
old
and in need of a bedtime story (no one is here to read
to me).
I convince myself I'm not lonely at all,
measuring out breaths like they are heartbeats.
I've done this all before, I remind myself…all those
years ago.
And I'll do it over and over until death takes me with
her.

Vessel

How do I tell you your cum wakes me in the night.
I sit on the toilet checking e-mails on my phone,
probe for new Instagram likes (of which there are
none at 3am).
It squeezes out of me protesting each release.
Your three second gratification lingers in my body for
two moons.
You are the dog who takes a shit on the neighbor's
lawn,
then walks away, nose tipped high in the air.

Internal Dialogue

I paint nails
violet to twin
our handcuff set,
perch expectant on
edge of the bed
waiting for you to call me
a good girl,
stroke my cheek,
raise blood to kiss your fingertip.

I slip on
maroon thong
and feel it swishing
between cheeks.
As we walk to meet your friends
I wonder if they know the
deeds I'm going to
expose your body to
when we retreat into the
upstairs bathroom during dessert.

I shave myself
slippery—
a waterpark
to fulfill your
wildest desires.
A renovated
resort with so many

upgrades your eyes
don't know where to land.
As with all amusement rides…
the price of admission is never free.

When Daddy Says No

It's easy to feel like a discarded food wrapping
tossed out the window,
caught by the wind.
Having needs dismissed feels like
Thanksgiving leftovers sitting in the trash:
once a feast, now spoiled and left for the birds.

Aflame

I've asked for the paraffin candle
(again)
because my skin is still aflame
with his touch.
There is no treatment
that erases memory.
I metal scourge until every
old cell replenishes anew.
Rebirth this body in
other bodies of water to emerge pruned.
Maybe desire that singes flesh
under a newborn moon can
cure these festering ills.

How I Communicate Needs at 11:30PM

Maybe when I have needs that need meeting
I am standing alone on an island
and no planes are scheduled incoming.
Voice run hoarse from failed attempts to draw
your attention, a needle that cannot land the vein.

Sometimes I feel like I show up at a once crowded
airport
and there are no lines, no pilots, no planes…
just my bags and me.
Isolated in a foreign country and the signs
are symbols I cannot decipher.

If I put myself on the island, desolate yet wanting,
will you notice that I've disappeared? Watch me strip
every piece of cloth from body and dance
naked on sand. It's getting everywhere inside me
and only you can clean up this mess I've made.

Springtime Rain

Not so many years ago
my feverish words
were inflicted on
unsuspecting persons—
how quickly they became
allergic to my prose
and dashed for the door.
I need you to inhale them
like life support,
without them
your soul would perish
in a moment's quick breath.
Absorb my wounds
like a springtime rain,
let it recharge your direction.
If one day you wake and
the hunger dissipates,
leave while I am sleeping
so it all felt like a dream.

My Many Thanks

Sarah B, I wasn't ready to talk then, but I am now.

Mel, my person, thank you for the sex pillows. I will hide them in the apartment when your kids come to visit.

The Coven (Sarah, Emily, and Emily), thank you for showing me what true unconditional love is.

Adam (and Michael, deceased), thank you for your patience and at times much deserved harsh critique. You were the healthy balance I needed to forge my own path.

Karen, you stepped in to guide me when I was lost. You have a gift that cannot be measured in this realm.

Marie, thank you for waiving my copays for therapy when I couldn't afford them. Everyone should have access to mental healthcare.

Ravven, this book would not exist without your wisdom. You were the inspiration I've been waiting for many moons.

Daddy, thank you for all the attention. I'll be expecting a call after you read this. And maybe some chocolates too.

To the LGBT+ community—they hate us 'cause they ain't us.

Aimee Nicole is a chronically ill, queer poet currently residing in Rhode Island. She holds a BFA in Creative Writing from Roger Williams University and has been published by various lit mags. She is a poet on staff for Chasing Shadows Magazine. For fun, she enjoys attending roller derby bouts and trying desperately to win at drag bingo. Her first collection, *Daily Worship*, was published by Laughing Ronin Press in January of 2022. This is her second book.